DISCARD

9-01

Running Back to Ludie

Also by Angela Johnson

NOVELS
Humming Whispers

Songs of Faith

Toning the Sweep

POETRY
The Other Side: Shorter Poems

PICTURE BOOKS
The Aunt in Our House

Daddy Calls Me Man

Do Like Kyla

The Girl Who Wore Snakes

Julius

The Leaving Morning

One of Three

The Rolling Store

Shoes like Miss Alice's

Tell Me a Story, Mama

The Wedding

When I Am Old with You

BOARD BOOKS
Joshua by the Sea

Joshua's Night Whispers

Mama Bird, Baby Birds

Rain Feet

Angela Johnson

Running Back to Ludie

illustrated by Angelo

Orchard Books / New York

An Imprint of Scholastic Inc.

All rights reserved. Published by Orchard, an imprint of
Scholastic Inc. ORCHARD BOOKS and design are registered
trademarks of Orchard Books, Inc., a subsidiary of Scholastic Inc.
SCHOLASTIC and associated logos are trademarks and/or
registered trademarks of Scholastic Inc.

Library of Congress Cataloging-in-Publication Data
Johnson, Angela.
Running back to Ludie / by Angela Johnson ; illustrated by
Angelo.—lst ed.
    p.   cm.
ISBN 0-439-29316-2 (alk. paper)
l. African American families—Juvenile poetry. 2. African American
girls—Juvenile poetry. 3. Mothers and daughters—Juvenile poetry.
4. Maternal deprivation—Juvenile poetry. 5. Children's poetry,
American. [1. Mothers and daughters—Fiction. 2. African
Americans—Fiction. 3. American poetry.] I. Angelo, date, ill.
II. Title.
PS3560.O37129   R8   2001   811'.54—dc21   2001-016298

10 9 8 7 6 5 4 3 2 1   01 02 03 04 05

Printed in the U.S.A.   37
First edition, October 2001
This book is set in 10.5 Leawood Book.
Book design by Mina Greenstein

For Jaye Horvath

—A.J.

For the brothers two,

Amier and Brandon

—A.

Contents

Running Back to Ludie

Strolling

I remember the way
the sidewalk looked when
I was being pushed
over
it
quickly.
And I remember the way
milk would freeze up on
my face when I got strolled
out into the cold.
Everybody calls it false memory
and having dreams of an imaginary
mother.
But I just go down to the basement,
touch my old stroller,
and smile.

Lucille

My friends have mothers,
I have Aunt Lucille.
I wear Lucille's
old dresses that have
glitter and spangles all over.
Bad seventies clothes, she says
but they flow and move
in
the
breeze
of the box fan in my window
when I stand on the bed.
And sometimes I think
('cause there's no other woman around)
maybe I look
just
like
her.
Except for
the way
she puts her hands on her hips
when somebody says something dumb.

3

Me and Vicki Freeman dropped
a tomato off the roof of the school
and had detention until
my Aunt Lucille said,
 "No more of this silly crap,"
'cause she was tired of picking me
up after all the buses had gone.
Tired from being on the phone
at work all day,
and tired of me and Vicki complaining
about everything
and feeling like nobody
understood us or how
incredible we truly are—making tomato art.
When Aunt Lucille rolls her eyes,
I shrug and wonder what she
expects from girls who
throw tomatoes
from roofs.

A Tea

The invitation said,
A tea for Mothers and Daughters.
I didn't even tell Lucille about it
and threw the envelope into the garbage
can beside the TV in Dad's office.
And I was happy when he found it
and looked like he might cry.
I'd stopped crying about being mom-free
but had to make sure nobody forgot it—
and in the end wound up with Dad holding
a tea cup and cookies on his knees,
talking with women
about dress sizes and their husbands.

Lavender

I open the
envelope to
lavender whiffs
of purple paper
and
smooth round writing
that says
"I've missed you
and see your eyes when I wake up
and look in the mirror."
And

"Has it been too long?"
For me to love her
and let her be my
mother.
After colds, stitches, and
other small child hurtings
and longings
with my father and aunt
beside me.
I breathe deep the
lavender, leaning
against my father
and whisper,
"No—not too long . . ."

Running Back to Ludie

There's a video of me running
through the park
when I was
two,
looking back at my mom, Ludie.
I run from her like I want
her to follow me
through
the
wildflowers I dive into.
I run from her like
I want her to feel the
scratchy flower stems and smell
the lavender I land on.
The video ends there and
I can't remember if
I ran back to her—
or if she followed.

Boulders

If you rolled a
fifty ton boulder
through the neighborhood where I live
and the suburbs next to us,
all the people together would
run screaming down the street
and have to brush up against
people they don't like because of
their cars, what they eat and
the
color
of their skin.
I need a boulder.

Underground Railroad

I live on an old street
that everybody says
used to have two houses
that were part of the Underground Railroad.
And before I learned that it really wasn't
a train,
I used to listen for the whistle
in the middle of the night
and thought about how I would
have thrown sandwiches and blankets
to the escaping slaves.
Riding to freedom.

keeping Warm

When my dad said
that I could visit Ludie
he left the house
walking real fast (which is what he does when he
wants to think).
I went after him
to ask him when—
but he was already running up the street
just as the lights were
coming on over our street.
But all I could think was
that he needed a coat to
keep him warm in the setting
sun, and how he might
be thinking how he doesn't want to share me.

There was this box of pictures that
for some reason (on a rainy day)
I felt I should float down the
storm sewer in front of our house.
They were old pictures of people I didn't
know and places I couldn't remember ever going.
But just as they were floating away to gone and
gone forever, I thought they might be missed
someday by somebody.
Somebody.
I decided not to float them.
I decided to let them stay in the box
of stuff marked LUDIE'S THINGS.
When I put them back, I taped the box up
to keep it all safer from girls like me
who one day might want to float something.

Cracks

I don't step

on

cracks.

Ever.

I walk with

my head down.

Watching.

More careful than the others

with

mothers

that they take for granted.

Mr. Charles Vivien

Mr. Charles Vivien (next door)
never leaves his yard
and keeps guns all over his house,
Aunt Lucille says.
She says he doesn't think
it's safe outside his yard.
Mr. Vivien grows his own food
and couldn't even bring himself
to go to his only relative's funeral.

But he throws softballs back to us
that we lose in his yard
and shares tomatoes with us
over the fence.
I wonder how long Mr. Vivien
will feel this way.

Grapes

I might like grapes as much as I do
    (my dad says)
because my mom ate them all the time
while she was pregnant.
She couldn't get enough
and even had Dad put a grape
arbor up in the backyard.
She used to sit under it, he said,
and listen to me.
I sit under it now and try
to imagine
what she would say
as she listened to me now.

Love

I went with Vicki and her brother Mac to get a tattoo.
Not for me,
or
Vicki.
Just Mac.
Even though I sometimes wonder if he's got any sense
at all.
Nothing pretty about getting a tattoo.
Me and Vicki drank Snapples and cried,
Mac's tattoo hurt us so bad.
And I wonder how bad it hurt him
'cause you know a senior in high school
isn't going to cry
in front of his little sister
and a girl that has loved him
all her silent heart life.

There's this old woman
who sits under the bridge downtown
and fishes all day.
I've seen a real young guy carry
her to her spot from an old beat-up
station wagon.
Her
eyes
twinkled
that day he gently put her down
at the willow by the river.
And I thought, yeah,
she's still fishing.
And I wanted to start doing like her.
When I started talking bait and fishing to Dad,
he just smiled at me,
overworked and tired.
But a week later he watched *Bassmasters*
with me and talked about
getting a canoe.

Camera

There is a picture of Ludie
dancing in a T-shirt and
high-top tennis shoes.
She must have been about my age
when somebody hid behind
a tree and stole the moment from
her.
Twisting
and
twirling.
Dancing.
There is a picture of
me,
standing in a T-shirt
with no shoes.
Aunt Lucille is trying
to get me to smile.
My heart twists and twirls
and all I can think
about is how I want her
to close the shutter
and let me dance.

I got my hair cut
because I did not want to meet Ludie
again looking like
the baby she left with a head
full
of curls.
So I watched somebody (through the mirror)
named Tiffany or Chiffon (who smelled like
    cotton candy)
clip,
clip,
my hair and talk about the party
she went to the night before
and where she'd be going on vacation.
I sat in the doctor's office
and talked about
how I felt about Ludie,
what I thought about Ludie,
and what I might expect from Ludie,
until my head hurt and neck ached.

And the doctor said my dad
was worried about what was
in my head about it all.
Clip,
clip.

Driving

Dad taught me to drive
a stick shift on the beaches off of Lake Erie.
Aunt Lucille sat in the back
laughing and eating
cheese crackers,
while I watched the waves
more than the steering wheel.
Got stuck
more than I drove.
Ludie taught my dad to drive
(right on the beach too).
He'd driven right into the water (then)
wave-watching like me,
'cause he'd heard once that you
shouldn't turn your back to the sea.

So when I drove into the lake

and we had to be towed,

instead of screaming,

he laughed

and said there was nothing like driving

on the water,

driving into the sea.

Man

Dad says when he was ten a carnival
came to town.
Put a tent around a box with a
frozen man
in it.
Called him the *Prehistoric Frozen Man.*
And Dad says he thought it would
be this man in skins holding a club.
Frozen.
But it turned out to be
some old miner who'd been
caught in an ice flow.

Not prehistoric at all.

Just so sad, that it made Dad

cry and wonder when they'd stop showing

him for fifty cents and let him rest.

He walked home kicking the dirt

and never went back to a carnival again.

That more than anything told me

I was his child.

The Only One

Vicki has six brothers
and their house vibrates in the evening
with radio sounds
and yelling from floor
to
floor.
I sit on their stairs
and drink the house in
between dinner with tons
of food and so much talk and
laughter it almost becomes
one loud food-filled yell.
And it isn't like home
where sometimes (if everybody is working late)
I'm the only one
eating at our kitchen table,
and only the sound of the ceiling fan
spins against the quiet.

Dog

I used to talk about having one.
A dog.
I'd call him something like
Sonny or Mike and he'd wear a
bandanna and catch Frisbees in the park.
But my cousin Rachel said her brother
Jake did all those things and more and the
family wouldn't mind if I took him off their hands
and changed his name.
I guess Rachel never will understand the
idea behind pets.

Flecks

I haven't stolen plums since I heard
everybody talking about how you shouldn't
go into the Flecks' backyard.
The story is,
some guy did (nobody knows his name)
and never came back.
And even though our neighborhood
is full of liars
and the Flecks just laugh
when somebody mentions the missing guy,
I don't think my need for plums is worth it.

Traffic

Didn't get to fly on a plane
till I was seven
and then I couldn't get over how Dad ate peanuts,
relaxed,
and didn't complain about traffic,
or
If we should leave at
3:00 A.M. to miss the traffic
or
Could we have taken a different road to
bypass the traffic.
I now can say—

(No) No one packed for me.

(No) No one asked me to carry anything for them.

(No) I never left my bag alone.

Which bugs me and sometimes makes me want to get up at 3:00 A.M. and dodge traffic with relatives.

Coming Back to Ludie

My mother lives in a cabin in the woods
that says
Sit with me by the fire . . .
            (We'll have hot chocolate)
Please.
And her hands are warm on my face
as she walks me to the front room
full of quilts and firelight.
She'd smiled at my dad
as he stepped back off the porch
into what was.

Daughter

They all say,
"She looks just like you, Elaine."
And I remember everybody she
used to know only
calls her Ludie.
I must be Elaine's daughter
as we walk
side by side
past country stores and restaurants.
I must be Elaine's daughter
as she points at this and laughs at that.
I must be Elaine's daughter
because we swing our arms the same
as we walk into the sunlight.
So when we walk by
a big window and my reflection glints off
into the street,
Elaine's daughter looks right back at me.

Suddenly

I look at Ludie and think
it is not a bad thing to all of a
sudden
miss what you
could have had.
Because the could-have-had
was not going to be as good as
I dreamt it.

But the coulds make my stomach
hurt and the whole room
cold,
even under the warm firelight
and the warm smiles Ludie gives me.

Pictures

There are pictures of
people I do not know
on all of Ludie's tables.
They smile
and hug the people next
to them.
And I remember how the same
pictures (different people)
are what I wake up to
every day of my life.
Makes me look at her and
wonder
where
she's been; living a life
with people who are
not
me.

Super Girl

I used to be a super girl.
Everybody said so.
Leap tall buildings in a single bound
and always said
thank you to my
elders.
Carried bags for people
who couldn't
and saved cats out
of trees on bright
summer days.
Always brushed my teeth after meals too
'cause the super girl manual said so.
But it's hard staying a super girl.
And sometimes no good deed goes unpunished.
I used to be a super girl.

In Two Parts (Again)

The doctor wonders if there
is something on my mind
because a teacher told my dad
(who usually doesn't listen)
that I don't pay attention
and I don't join in.
Which makes me wonder
why the teacher isn't talking to the doctor
about feeling
rejected
by a junior high girl.
Whack.
Lucille says
I should let my
hair
grow.
While getting foot long
nails glued to her hands
and listening to
(cotton candy girl)
say they really liked my old curls
and maybe I should think

about growing them back,
'cause what was isn't exactly
always bad.
Whack,
whack.
I don't feel that much about
me and Ludie has changed,
but it feels good to
sit on the doctor's couch
and show
my new short
hair to her.
Then she will know
I'll never have a problem
letting go.

Nightmares

Got dared to spray paint
the bridge downtown,
hanging upside down
like everybody else did.
But I had nightmares of falling
headfirst
into the river,
embarrassed to death
if I had to be taken to the hospital
with a can in my hand

and my dress over my head.

Now I believe like some say.

You can work some of the hard things

out in your dreams.

Or just chalk the sidewalks in front

of your house.

Mick and June

Never did understand twins very much
so I'm always watching
Mick and June.
Who look exactly alike,
laugh at everything together,
move the same,
and almost seem to try to be each
other.
Nobody can tell them apart,
not even their parents
who call them "twin"
like they are one person
in Geranimal clothes.
But even then I sometimes wonder what it would be
like to wake up in the
morning and see me in the bathroom
before I even got there.

Out of the Woods

Our house feels
different
now that I have
been to the
woods.
I move around it
sitting on the couch
wondering if anything
will be like it was.
I get the crazy cold shakes
that something lives
with me, Lucille, and Dad
that won't
leave us like we were.
But then the cold shakes
are gone
and I know
they are a leftover
from not having Ludie
at all.

43

List

I used to keep a list of the
people that I loved in this world.
Numbered it.
Changed it.
Would lie across my bed
and think about
how long the list would get
and if I'd need more paper.
Sometimes I'd go weeks
and not look at it.
But then I'd get what
Vicki's mom calls
"heart stir"
and look at it again.

Lost the list in a
snowstorm last year
running home almost frozen to
Aunt Lucille (who got off work early),
Dad (two minutes behind me),
and all the things
that reminded me of who I
loved
and why they
were on the list
anyway.

Guess

I used to guess
about everything
and was
always the winner
when somebody said
"Guess what?"
But only found out later
that they didn't really mean
"Guess,"
only
"I got
something to tell
you won't believe."
And always wondered after that
why people don't just say
what
they
mean.

Perfect

There are these kids
I know who walk
like they know about
everything
in the whole damned world that's
perfect.
And most of the time the
world tells them
they're probably right.
You could fill
an ocean with what
I don't know.
And I watch them
sometimes and wonder
what it would take
for me to
walk like them.

After

The days after Ludie
were just that;
days.
Put my shoes on the
same and still
thought mashed potatoes
were good.
But slowly I started
to make room for
her in my Grrls Address Book
and on my Christmas
list.
Put a picture of her
smiling into the sun on my
corkboard
and even mentioned her to
some kids I didn't know that well.
When I came back from Ludie's
my dad smiled.

A lot.
And talked till I fell asleep
warm on the couch, glad to be
home,
but thinking
after
about the next time
I'd go back to Ludie.